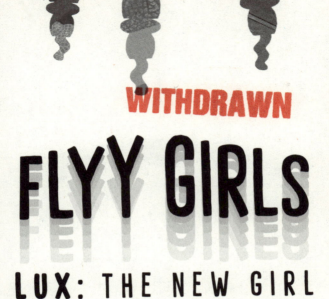

WITHDRAWN

FLYY GIRLS

LUX: THE NEW GIRL

BY ASHLEY WOODFOLK

PENGUIN WORKSHOP

PENGUIN WORKSHOP
An Imprint of Penguin Random House LLC, New York

Text copyright © 2020 by Ashwin Writing LLC. Illustrations copyright © 2020 by Penguin Random House LLC. All rights reserved. Published by Penguin Workshop, an imprint of Penguin Random House LLC, New York. PENGUIN and PENGUIN WORKSHOP are trademarks of Penguin Books Ltd, and the W colophon is a registered trademark of Penguin Random House LLC. Printed in the USA.

Visit us online at www.penguinrandomhouse.com.

Cover illustration by Zharia Shinn

Library of Congress Cataloging-in-Publication Data is available upon request.

ISBN 9780593096017 (pbk)   10 9 8 7 6 5 4 3 2 1
ISBN 9780593096024 (hc)   10 9 8 7 6 5 4 3 2 1

Lux Ruby Lawson was *not* having it. Not today, of all days.

But Simone Harding hadn't gotten the message. She was trying Lux's patience, the way she always did, and Lux didn't know how much longer she could listen to Simone's loud, whiny voice.

"She thinks she's so cute," Lux heard Simone say. "Just because she's the new girl. Well, I've been at this school and on this team since we were freshmen. I've paid my dues. And I'm not going to let some *nobody* who came out of *nowhere* try to take this away from me."

Simone was the speed jumper on their school's double Dutch team—one of the most coveted positions. Lux had tried out for the team that day, along with about a dozen other girls, but she didn't actually care what position she got. She just needed something that would keep her out of trouble. Something to *do*—besides cranking her music as loud as she could stand it. Or taking photos of random people on the street to keep from being so pissed off all the time. (*Pissed* had been her default setting ever since her dad left.)

And after the last . . . incident, her mom had warned her. If she messed up again, she'd have to go live with the dad who'd walked out on her. Lux couldn't let that happen.

This was her final chance to make things right.

But Simone kept talking crap about her—she'd been tormenting Lux since Lux started at this school last semester. To make matters worse, Lux's dad had called that morning. He told her she had a new baby sister, Lillia Rose—a sibling she hadn't asked for and didn't want. A daughter he'd chosen to stay with when it seemed so easy for him to leave *her*. Lillia felt like Lux's replacement, no matter what anyone said.

And Simone still wouldn't shut the hell up.

Lux turned to look at the girl she had hated almost instantly.

Simone was tall, thin, and brown-skinned, with waist-length braid extensions, and Lux had been wanting to yank the fake hair from her scalp for months. On Lux's very first day, Simone had tried her—walking up to her in the hall and making fun of the shirt she had on. Lux resisted the urge to grab her then. She couldn't start a fight on her first day. For most of the fall, Lux kept to herself and kept her distance, but now that winter had arrived, her patience was wearing thin.

Though Lux had moved away from Simone and her friends in the gym so she wouldn't hear whatever they were saying about her now, soon the coach called them all together again.

"Okay," the coach started. "I'd like to see Aisha, Penelope, Tamika, and Lux back here for practice tomorrow. Thanks to everyone else for coming out."

Simone glared. But Lux grinned. She couldn't help it if she was good—better than Simone, even—and the coach saw her potential.

But back in the locker room, things went wrong . . . fast.

Simone stepped right into Lux's face the second the coach left. "You think you're such hot shit, don't you?"

Lux stayed calm at first. She shook her head and turned away from Simone, even as Simone's friends egged her on. Everyone knew that Lux had transferred here because she'd gotten kicked out of her last school for fighting, and she'd heard that Simone and her friends were dying to see if she could live up to her reputation.

Lux wouldn't give them what they wanted. She opened her locker like Simone wasn't even there. But then her phone chimed, and she saw another picture of Lillia. The newborn had the same rich dark skin as Lux, the same thick black hair. She looked soft and new and not yet ruined. And just as Lux hit the power button on her phone, Simone grabbed her wrist and spun Lux around to face her again. Lux's phone hit the floor and the screen cracked.

"I'm talking to you," Simone snapped.

And that was all Lux could take.

The sound a fist makes when it's hitting a nose is horrible.

It sounds like . . . a wet kind of crunch.

It reminded Lux of the sound her mouth made as she bit into one of her favorite snacks, Cool Ranch Doritos.

But in that moment, as Lux's closed fist slammed into Simone's nose, Lux could only think about shutting Simone up.

Simone's body smacked the floor with more force than Lux's phone had. And before Lux knew it, she'd climbed on top of her and began pounding her fists into the other girl's face and chest and stomach.

"Holy–!" someone shouted.

Simone reached for Lux's thick twists, grabbed a few of them, and pulled, yanking Lux's head painfully forward. Lux thought, *Oh no this girl didn't*. A second later she thought, *I should have done that first*. But she wasn't worried. Like jumping double Dutch, fighting was something Lux did well.

"Oh my God!" someone else said. Girls from every part of the locker room had shoved into the aisle where Lux and Simone were rolling around on the floor.

Lux grabbed Simone's hair right back, ignoring the sting of her own screaming scalp. She punched Simone again, so hard her knuckles cracked.

"Jesus!" said another voice. Then, "Luxy, no!"

That voice Lux recognized. It belonged to Danika, the only girl who had been kind to her when she came to this school at the start of fall semester. The two grew closer after Lux had protected Danika from a group of bullies back in November—Lux told the girls who were tormenting Danika that if they kept it up, they'd have to deal with her. And when Danika found Lux crying in the bathroom right after she'd found out her dad's new wife was pregnant, she'd stayed with her and handed her fistfuls of crumpled toilet tissue until she'd calmed down.

But none of that mattered now.

Lux looked up at Danika, intent on telling her not to worry about coming to her rescue, but in that one distracted second, Simone shoved Lux so hard, she fell backward. Her head hit the row of lockers behind them.

That's when Lux noticed the phones. Almost every girl in the locker room had been taking photos of her, videos of them. And Lux knew that they would be shared again and again for hundreds of other eyes to see. Normally, Lux loved cameras—they were one of her most favorite things. But she hated everything about this. Simone scrambled up and away from her.

"You're a psychopath!" Simone shouted. Her nose wouldn't stop bleeding. Droplets of blood were falling onto her shirt. One of Simone's friends grabbed her arm to hold her back.

"She's not worth it, S," the friend said, then she hissed in Lux's direction, "This isn't over." Lux felt pretty sure this girl, Bree, only made empty threats—Lux had seen her acting like Simone's bodyguard more than once. But the look in Bree's eyes still gave Lux goose bumps. She could imagine Simone, Bree, and the rest of them cornering her. But Lux knew they didn't have the nerve to do anything else now, not with so many people watching.

The coach ran in, but by then everything had ended. Bree was still holding Simone back, and Lux still sat on the concrete floor, but they were both refusing to speak.

"Luxy," Danika said again, softly, from somewhere behind her. Lux felt Danika touch her shoulder, but she pushed her sort-of friend's hand away.

"Just leave me alone," Lux said to her. She couldn't remember the last time she'd had a friendship that felt anywhere close to real.

"Get changed and get to class," Coach said to all the other girls. And this is how Lux knew Danika didn't really care: She seemed to hesitate for a second, but she left with everyone else.

Lux picked up her ruined phone and saw

that her nail polish was chipped, too. She glared at Simone and smoothed down her hair.

"You two," Coach continued, pointing to Lux and Simone, "come with me."

3

"Expelled," Principal Bower said.

The word rang through Lux's brain like an alarm she couldn't shut off.

"Expelled," her mother repeated, and it sounded like acceptance more than shock. After all, this had already happened to Lux twice in the year since her dad had packed up, left, and started his new family. She'd always had a short temper, but in the last ten months it had gotten so much worse.

Principal Bower nodded. "We have a zero-tolerance policy when it comes to fighting," he said. He slid a thin blue booklet across the table, flipped it open, and pointed to something he'd highlighted about halfway down the page. "It's outlined clearly in our student handbook, and all students are required to sign the last page upon enrollment." He flipped to the back and pointed to Lux's signature—two loopy *L*s with a scribble between them. She'd barely read the booklet before signing it on her third day at this school just a few months ago. Principal Bower looked sternly over his glasses at Lux and then her mother.

"You could say it's our version of a contract," he said. "And I've seen enough of the altercation on the phones of various students, as well as speaking with a few of the kids who were in the locker room. Lux threw the first punch."

Genevieve Lawson sighed. "I can't believe this," she said. "Again, Lux?" When Lux just kept staring at her chipped manicure, Genevieve grabbed her daughter's chin and turned her head hard to face her. "I'm done, okay? I told you that you had one more chance, and you blew it."

Lux flared her nostrils and crossed her arms. Then she uncrossed them when her mother gave her *the look*. "Yeah," Lux said. "I know." Her mother dropped her hand from Lux's face, and Lux stared through the dirty window behind Principal Bower's head at the busy Brooklyn sidewalk. The two adults kept talking, and Lux wished she could go outside with her camera.

"Let's go," Genevieve said, and by the sound of her voice, Lux knew she'd be getting an earful in the car. "Thank you for your time, Mr. Bower."

As they stood to leave, Lux's phone chimed.

Another text from her father.

So when do you want to come visit your new baby sister?

Little did he know she'd soon be coming to stay.

4

Luke Lawson II lived in a doorman building with his new family. It was only a few subway stops from the tiny Brooklyn walk-up where he'd lived with Lux and her mom for sixteen years, but it seemed worlds away. A few days after her expulsion, Lux stood staring up at the building. It was modern and made mostly of glass. She could see Hispanic families making dinner and young white couples watching TV. The building hid nothing, but it made her want to hide.

Lux's dad had been furious when her mom

called him to explain their daughter's latest fight—so mad, in fact, that he didn't want to speak to Lux at all. Lux overheard her mother's half of the conversation from her bedroom, though, her ear pressed to the wall.

"I'm just as pissed as you are, Luke," Genevieve said. "But she's clearly out of control . . . No. We are *not* sending our daughter to military school. Absolutely not . . . My friend is the vice principal at an arts school over in Harlem. I can try to pull some strings . . . What she needs is a fresh start, and a firmer hand than mine . . . I *know* you just had a baby. But your *other* daughter needs you, too."

Now, Lux nodded to the uniformed man holding open the door, hating everything about where she'd ended up. And after she gave her name at the front desk, before she'd even made it into the elevator, she knew she'd hate living in this snooty place, too.

"Are you new to the building?" a narrow-shouldered white woman asked Lux, her high-heeled boots clicking as she walked over. She looked at Lux's sneakers, her beaded twists, her pin-covered backpack, and her beat-up suitcase as if nothing about her belonged there.

Lux tossed her hair over her shoulder and pulled her headphones from her ears, settling them around her neck. "Yeah," Lux said, and left it at that. She didn't owe this woman anything. After stepping into the elevator, she punched the button for her dad's floor and texted him, *I'm on my way up.*

"Well, *I've* never seen you here before," the woman said, tucking her red hair behind her ears.

Lux looked at her and blinked. "So?" Lux replied.

"Which apartment do you live in?" the woman continued, and Lux shook her head, getting more and more pissed by the minute. She couldn't stop the heat spreading across her chest and rising up the back of her neck. Why did people insist on *trying* her at the worst possible moments?

"Look, lady. Chill out. I'm not gonna screw up your day. How about you don't screw with mine?"

The woman stretched her blue eyes wide. And when the elevator arrived on the seventh floor, Lux stepped into the hall without looking back.

❧❧

Newborn babies are loud.

Lux could hear the kid before her father

even opened his front door. Once he did, and Lux stepped inside, she immediately slipped her headphones firmly back in place, hoping they'd cancel out some of the noise.

"Luxana," her father said, calling her by the full name she despised. She hadn't seen him in nearly four months and she'd forgotten about his salt-and-pepper goatee, his broad shoulders and thick eyebrows. Something inside her softened the tiniest bit. He smiled crookedly for only a second as he reached out and pulled her into a half hug with one of his arms.

"Take those headphones off," he said, and slowly, Lux did. He took her suitcase and told her she should take off her shoes before stepping farther inside. "Lillia and Penny are in the baby's room. She's trying to get her to go down for a nap."

Missed you, too, Dad, Lux thought but didn't say.

She followed him down the hall, and he turned into a small room. When he first moved away, he told her he got a place with three bedrooms so she could have her own space if she wanted to come stay for the weekend or longer. But this was the first time Lux had stepped foot inside the apartment. For all their visits so far, she'd just asked him to meet her at a park or a store, or he'd taken her out to dinner and given her money for a taxi home at the end of the night. Once Penny started the last trimester of her pregnancy, he felt anxious about leaving her, so Lux hadn't seen him at all.

The room had three bare white walls and a twin-size bed covered with purple sheets. A floor-to-ceiling glass window made up the fourth wall. Lux felt exposed inside the room and somehow trapped at the same time. She flopped down on the bed and tossed her backpack onto the floor. She turned away from her dad to look through the window.

"Hang that on the hook in the closet," Luke said instantly. "I know how things were at your mom's, but you're not going to just do whatever you want to here."

Her father couldn't have been more wrong. Lux's mom hadn't changed—she ruled their home with the same iron fist she always had. The only difference now was that he was gone.

Lux couldn't stop reimagining the day he left. The way he'd barely looked at her the night before; the way she'd woken up to find him and all his things gone without warning. He disappeared, like a coward, and now she finally knew why. He'd decided this random woman, this *Penny*, was much more important to him than his actual family.

Lux picked up her bag. She hung it on the hook he pointed out. And in that moment she realized her life here would be a lot more difficult.

"Hang up your jacket, too, and then come into the baby's room to say hello to Penny. Dinner's at eighteen hundred hours. Your mother made some calls, pulled some strings. You have an interview at Augusta Savage School of the Arts in the morning. Be ready by oh seven hundred."

Military time. Lux had forgotten her dad's old habit from his time as a marine. He left the room then, and Lux felt her eyes start to sting—a sure sign of tears. But she wouldn't let herself cry again today.

"Ugh," she whispered, taking in her harsh new reality.

Before leaving her old apartment, she'd cried

and begged to stay and promised her mom that she would change. But her mom just said, "I can't do this with you anymore, Lux." Lux hoped that if she could stay out of fights and avoid trouble for the rest of the semester, then maybe she could move back home.

❄

The baby's room was small and dark, lit only by an elephant-shaped night-light. Penny, Lux's new stepmom, sat in a rocking chair in a far corner of the room. Lux waved.

Penny smiled. She was curvy and light-skinned, with fluffy brown hair she always pushed back with a headband, and she had on a tight pair of yoga pants. Even though she'd only just had this baby two weeks ago, Lux could imagine the grossest boys in her old class calling Penny a MILF.

"This is your baby sister, Lillia," Penny said softly, turning a little so Lux could see the face of the sleeping baby. Lux had met Penny only once before, so she felt like a complete stranger, and though the kid looked cute, it didn't change anything. It definitely didn't make Lux think of either of them as family. She felt heat creep up her neck the way it always did before she said or did something she regretted, so she knew she needed an excuse to get away from them fast.

"I gotta go get unpacked," Lux said. "But I'll see you at dinner, I guess?"

Penny looked a little disappointed, but Lux didn't have it in her to get any closer, to coo at or cuddle with the kid.

Back in her room, Lux sat on the bed and scrolled through her phone. She saw photos of Bree and Simone and the rest of the girls from her old school, and it pissed her off that they hadn't gotten in trouble, but her whole life had changed. A minute later, she decided to unfollow everyone who went to her old school. She needed a fresh start, and dwelling on the past wouldn't help her move on.

Lillia wailed loudly in the next room, so Lux put her headphones on again and turned her music way up before lying down on her bed. As she rolled over onto her stomach and got ready to hit the unfollow button on someone else's page, she got a notification that she'd been tagged.

She tapped through to see what it could be, and then she froze. She watched as the on-screen version of herself climbed on top of Simone Harding and began hitting her over and over again.

Lux sat straight up, then jumped out of bed.

She paced from her big, too-bright window to her bedroom door and back. She played the video again and again, cringing at her on-screen self. She almost didn't believe she had that kind of rage inside her.

"Dammit." She didn't know what would happen if this spread the way these fight videos sometimes did. But she knew *exactly* what would happen if her father saw the video—she could kiss the possibility of moving back in with her mother goodbye.

She tried to figure out if someone watching the video would recognize her. Her dark brown skin could be seen pretty clearly, and so could the twists she always wore with the wooden beads at the ends. But her face never showed up front and center. From this angle, she tried to tell herself, she could have been any black girl in Brooklyn.

She soothed herself with this half-truth as she untagged herself. Then she sat on the edge of her bed and continued to quietly panic. There were at least twenty girls in that locker room, and more than half of them took photos and videos of that fight. Lux wondered if anyone else would post it. She wondered if anyone important would *see* it. She wondered if she'd be untagging herself for the rest of her life.

When her dad called her to dinner, she went and ate everything on her plate, making polite conversation with Penny, even though it made her feel like a huge phony.

But after dinner, Lux played all of her favorite sad songs and cried like she had with her mother, staring through her new, huge window. She'd only been away from home for a few hours and already everything was falling apart. She wished she'd never punched

Simone. She hated to admit it, but she wanted her mom.

When she calmed down, she dried her eyes and pulled out her camera. She took photo after photo of the still-twinkling lights of the city until she got too tired to stand. And just before she fell asleep, she pulled out her phone to text her mom.

I hate it here. I want to come home.

Genevieve texted back a few minutes later. *I'm sorry, honey. I really am. But you should have thought about that before you got into that fight.*

—February 20—

I'm at Dad's. It sucks.

Lillia is loud, and Dad is being a jerk, and I hope Penny knows she'll never be my mom.

I need to get out of here.

I also can't believe that someone would tag me in that video. I mean, who does that? And since Dad's always talking about how I gotta work extra hard as a black woman to make sure I'm representing myself well, he CANNOT find out about it. Something like this—physical proof that I'm not the perfect, disciplined kid he wants everyone to think I am—is his worst nightmare. I heard Mom talking to him about military school, and I could SO see him sending me away if he sees that video.

I just need to keep my head down, stay

outta trouble, and try to make this work till June so I can move back in with mom. But it's not gonna be easy.

I need a plan.

HOW I'm GOING TO GET THE HELL OUT OF HERE

1. Do whatever Dad says.
2. Get into that new school.
3. make GOOD friends. The kind of girls who don't get into trouble. The kind of girls who get good grades and have hobbies and that people like.
4. Join some kinda club or something. Joiners keep busy and don't have time for drama.
5. Stay AWAY from boys.
6. make sure no one knows about that video.

5

"So, Miss Lawson, tell me why it is you want to attend Augusta Savage School of the Arts."

Lux didn't feel like sucking up to these people. But she knew what she had to do to get out of her father's apartment, and acing this interview would be step one. (Knowing the only other option was military school definitely motivated her, too.) Once Lux had made her mind up about something, she couldn't be stopped—and she did nothing halfway. It was why she'd won nearly every single fight she'd ever been in. And why Simone Harding was walking around with a broken nose.

Lux cleared her throat and pulled an old photo album out of her backpack. She knew from reading the school's website last night that she needed to show them a portfolio, but she didn't have time to put together something like that, so this would have to do.

"I've loved photography for as long as I can remember," Lux said. She flipped through the album, showing off black-and-white portraits of old men and women playing chess at Washington Square Park, bright images of kids jumping into the white spray of water from open fire hydrants, and close-ups of sweet-faced pit bulls at the animal shelter where Lux liked to spend her Saturday mornings.

Her father sat beside her in front of the admissions board; a mean-looking bald man, a woman with a curly Afro, and a person with piercings up and down both their ears were staring back at them from a short table. They'd introduced themselves when Lux and her father first arrived, but Lux's nerves had already erased their names from her memory. Luke leaned forward to look at the album, too.

It felt like she'd opened up her heart for all four of them to see.

"I'm mostly self-taught," Lux continued, "but I'd love to learn real techniques." She flipped another page and noticed her hand shaking. She quickly tucked it into her lap. "You might have noticed I love taking portraits. I want to learn how to better capture people naturally. You know, when they're not posing or posed."

"Yes, I can see that," the woman with the Afro said. She smiled and pulled the album away from Lux, sliding it closer to their side of the table.

"How long have you been doing this kind of work?" the pierced admissions person asked.

"I got serious about it a year and a half ago. I started watching tutorials on YouTube and checking out books from the library about it. That kind of thing. But I probably took my first photo when I was ten. My grandpa gave me an old film camera and turned the closet under his stairs into a darkroom, just for me."

Lux swallowed hard and avoided her father's eyes. His dad had passed away a year and a half ago and left Lux all of his cameras. This explained how her mom knew she might want to go to a school where she could take pictures. But Lux wondered if her father had even remembered that she loved photography.

"We understand you were expelled from your last school for fighting," the woman with the Afro said next. "How do we know that behavior wouldn't happen here?"

Lux saw her dad tense in the chair next to her. He said, "She's living with me now. So it won't." Lux got annoyed that he'd spoken for her, but she took a deep breath and nodded.

"He's right, it won't, but not just because I'm living with him. I know I've run out of chances and options. So if things go badly here, I'll have nowhere else to go," she said firmly, looking at each of them. "I want this to be a real fresh start, and if you give me the chance to prove that I've changed, I won't let you down. I promise."

They all nodded, but they didn't seem convinced. Lux knew that her plea might not mean much to them, but she only made promises she planned to keep.

"Why should we accept you into Savage when there is a waiting list full of kids who have been working on their craft since they were in primary school?" the bald man asked next, with a frown. She looked squarely at the guy's bald head, and then at each of the piercings in the ears of the person next to him, and finally at the last woman's big, bushy hair. She thought about the last year—the divorce, the fights, the expulsions—and everything else that had gone wrong. This could be her opportunity to do something well and maybe even get something right.

She wanted to say that taking photos made it easier for her to breathe. But she worried that wouldn't make any sense. So she thought of something that would.

"There are probably five hundred photos in that album," Lux said. "And these are just Polaroids and pictures I shot with the film cameras I got from my grandfather." She reached into her bag and pulled out the digital camera she'd saved up for all last spring—the one she bought for cheap from a green-haired boy she'd fought another girl over, and then only spent the first month of summer kissing. "That doesn't include the hundreds I have on my DSLR"—she held the camera high—"or the thousands I have saved in the cloud. You should pick me because those kids that have been making art since they were five probably started doing it because someone made them. Someone else thought they should take ballet or learn to sing or play the damn violin or whatever." She hadn't meant to swear, but it slipped out, anyway. Her father barely flinched, but she knew she wouldn't hear the end of it once they were out of this office. She held her face still, didn't apologize, and kept talking. She had a point to make. "Those kids are probably living out their parents' failed dreams or something. But this?" Lux jabbed her finger in the direction of the photo album. "This all came directly from *me*."

Lux's heart wouldn't stop pounding after saying all that. She hadn't been that honest in months. And that's what scared her most of all—that she'd told the truth and they could still decide they didn't want her.

6

Lux woke up Monday morning to her father's voice spilling into her room.

"Luxana. Up. Be dressed and in the kitchen by oh seven hundred."

Lux groaned and looked at her clock. It was 6:45 a.m.

"You want me to be ready in *fifteen minutes*?" she whined. "Seriously? *What for*?"

"Look at the note on your desk."

Lux couldn't help it. She smiled at the ceiling before hopping out of bed.

Her dad used to leave her notes every

morning when they lived together. Silly drawings, funny quotes, sometimes just ones that said things like, *Shine today, Luxana Ruby Lawson*. She didn't think she'd ever get those notes back after he left. But maybe she was wrong.

Lux found a slip of yellow paper on her desk that read: *Got an email from Augusta Savage admissions late last night. You're in, baby girl! Good job.*

"I'm *what*?" Lux shouted, and she could hear her dad laughing from the kitchen.

As Lux stepped into the kitchen, she could tell her father had a big lecture/pep-talk/first-day-threat-sesh prepared. And Penny looked frazzled because Lillia was screaming. The whole scene seemed like it would stress Lux out. So she just grabbed a banana and got out of the apartment as quickly as possible, but she tucked the note into her pocket. Lux wanted to keep the glimpse of the old version of her dad with her.

On the way to school, she read over the list she'd written in her journal, made one small change, then she recited it over and over to the beat of the song blaring in her headphones. *Listen to Dad. Go to school. Make friends. Join a club. No boys.*

When she saw the school again, though, with its flying flags and murals along the doors, most of the list flew from her mind.

Lux hadn't noticed it when she came in for her interview, but Augusta Savage School of the Arts was in a short, colorful building, and it looked a little out of place. It sat squeezed between a dental office and a grocery store, on a tiny one-way street in Harlem. It seemed too cheerful and bright to belong on the otherwise gray block. Lux liked that about it she didn't feel like she fit in, either. She felt more excited than she wanted to admit. The school looked like it gave out second chances: a place where she might find *her* place. Lux had only one thought filling her head as she walked through the school's front doors. The final item on her list, she realized, was the most important one. *No one could know.*

No one could know the real reason she had to transfer in the middle of the year or what had happened at her old school. No one could know how often she got angry, or that videos and photos of her latest fight existed. No one could find out about Simone's broken nose. She'd been at enough schools to know that if people knew your history, you never got a real chance to start over.

She tried not to look lost or bring any attention to herself, but everyone else seemed to be doing the opposite. Lux noticed a rainbow's worth of dyed hair, too many piercings to count, and dozens of instrument-toting and wildly dressed students as she walked a short distance down the main hall. When she found her locker, she unzipped her backpack and used her phone's camera to check her makeup. Her pink lip gloss popped under the florescent lights. She looked good, she thought, especially for someone who'd only had fifteen minutes to get ready.

Lux opened her camera bag, checking to see which lenses she had with her. She didn't have some of the ones she might need, and she felt more amateurish than ever, but she turned to scan the hallway with her camera in hand. She hoped taking a few photos would help her feel calm, or at least more like herself.

"Hey," she heard a kinda cute guy say to her. "You dropped this." He was handing her a lens cap. His hazel eyes were peeking out from his gingerbread-brown face, and his messy charcoal-black hair made him look like trouble. Dark-haired guys were a weakness of hers, but boys were a complication she couldn't afford.

She could look, she told herself. She just wouldn't touch. "Thanks," she said, taking the cap from him and slipping it back into her camera bag. "Can I take your photo?"

He smirked and looked her up and down. Without blinking, she looked right back.

"Sure," he said. "You new?"

Lux shrugged and lifted her camera, loving

the weight of it. It made her feel invisible and seen all at once.

"Don't smile," she said, which always worked like a charm to break down whatever people tended to build in front of their faces the second they knew someone planned to take their picture.

The guy said, "What?" and laughed.

She snapped the photo. That single click eased a bit of tension out of her body. She wanted to take more pictures, but she didn't want him to think she was weird. She also worried he'd do something to piss her off and the whole turning-over-a-new-leaf thing she had going would be ruined on her first day. So she just said, "Thanks again."

She moved through the hall that way, using the camera to introduce and calm herself all at once. And she knew what they were thinking:

Who's the new girl taking pictures of whoever she wants? Where did she come from? And maybe even, *Who does she think she is?*

Lux sometimes wondered the same things about herself. In the past year, she'd tried being a loner, tried blending in, and tried fighting back. Now she would try being someone completely different. Someone likable. Someone who tried new things, and made friends, and who didn't get angry all the time. She hoped it would work.

●✕●

Just before first period, Lux found a copy of the school paper in the girls' bathroom. As she walked to class, she flipped through it, scanning the photos more than the articles themselves. She could see that the photographer had talent, but they kind of lacked . . . range. The photos, no matter the subject, were taken from far away. It made everything seem big and important, but Lux thought getting closer for certain moments might make the stories seem more personal and the students more human.

She thought that maybe, if given the chance, she could do better. *I do need to join a club,* she thought. And how perfect would being the newspaper photographer be? She imagined how she would have shot a story on the second page about the fine-arts students' last show.

When she looked up from the paper a second later, she spotted a group of pretty girls standing tall like they were royalty. They looked nothing like Danika or any of the other half-friends she'd had over the last year. They looked like they could be good for her—like the friends she had before her dad moved out, before she'd messed up at one school and then at another and her parents began to see her as a problem. Lux had been popular once, and popular girls were powerful. She had a feeling these girls were exactly what she needed to make sure what happened at her last school didn't happen here.

Lux stuffed the paper into her bag, pulled out her camera again, and walked toward them.

"Hey." She let her camera hang from one hand and reached out with the other. "I'm Lux," she said, knowing she only had one opportunity to make the right first impression. Her nails sparkled just the way she'd imagined they would when she picked this nail polish out of her collection before her interview. Genevieve Lawson taught her daughter that she could overcome anything with the right manicure. She hoped the nails would continue to serve her well.

One of the girls smiled at her. She was dark-skinned and curvy, with short relaxed hair cut into a bob, and she had on a skirt with flowers all over it. The lightest-skinned of the three, in ripped jeans and a shirt that hung off one of her freckled shoulders, watched Lux but didn't say anything. The last girl—the tallest and clearly the one in charge, the one Lux needed to impress—said, "Lux?" like she had misheard her.

Lux lowered her hanging hand and nodded. The way this girl looked at her made Lux feel all wrong—like she'd already messed things up.

The tall girl straightened her glasses, looked at her friends, then looked back at Lux. She sighed as if this whole conversation bored her, but then she said, "I'm Noelle. That's Tobyn, and Micah's the cute one in the skirt. You new? You seem new."

Lux stepped a little closer to them. "I am,"

she said. She lifted her camera and asked, "Can I take your photo?"

Noelle laughed. She doubled over and the tip of her high ponytail nearly touched the floor.

Micah smiled again. Tobyn frowned.

When Noelle stopped laughing, she said, "Well, that's pretty weird of you, Lux. But I can respect a girl with balls. And let's be real, we are pretty hot." She looped one arm around Tobyn's waist and flung the other over Micah's shoulders. The bright streak of blue in Tobyn's dark hair shone as she pushed out her lips, and Micah applied some gloss before smiling widely. They looked so damn perfect.

"Don't smile," Lux said.

Tobyn's lips slipped into a smirk. Micah's glossy mouth fell open in surprise. Noelle tilted her head to one side like she didn't know what to make of Lux.

Lux snapped the photo.

"Thanks," she said. "See you around?"

"Hope so," Micah said, grinning.

"For sure," Tobyn agreed.

"Looks like it," Noelle mumbled, turning back to the other girls. It felt like Noelle wanted to say that these were *her* friends and Lux could find her own. But Lux was determined. She needed friends, and these were the ones she wanted.

And when she put her mind to it, Lux always got what she wanted.

For the next two weeks, Lux mostly kept to herself, waving hi to the hazel-eyed boy when she saw him in the hall or in class (she'd learned his name was Emmett in one of the classes they had together) and talking to Tobyn and Micah whenever she bumped into them. She still hadn't cracked Noelle, but she had a lot of the same classes as her. She knew if she just waited for the right moment, played it cool, and didn't look too desperate, she might be able to wriggle her way into Noelle's good graces.

Lux's opportunity came when she least expected it. She noticed an open seat in her black-and-white photography class, right next to Noelle, and rushed to grab it. Noelle had moved her fingers a little in a not-quite wave when Lux walked in, and this simple gesture felt like progress. Lux took it as a sign.

"Okay, okay," Mr. Van Ness said from the front of the class. "I hope you all didn't have too much trouble with the homework. Let's just dive back in where we left off, shall we?"

Emmett took this class, too. Lux couldn't help but glance around for him. When her eyes found his, he raised his eyebrows at her, closed his open book so she could see the cover, and mouthed, *Page 146*. Lux didn't smile, but she wanted to. He'd caught her daydreaming last week during Mr. Van Ness's lecture and teased her about it after class, so he knew she wouldn't remember where they'd "left off."

Instead of reading along or listening, though, she rotated a little in her seat to talk to Noelle.

"You play cello, right?" Lux whispered.

Noelle rolled her eyes. "You know I play cello, weirdo." It was true. But Lux didn't know how else to start a conversation with a girl who seemed as angry at the world as she was. Noelle really didn't care what anyone thought of her, while Lux just pretended not to. Noelle made Lux feel like she was back in the school interview—Lux wanted to impress her, but she wished she didn't care so much.

"Right," Lux said with a smile. She shook her head. "What I meant was, *since* you play cello, why are you taking black-and-white film photography?"

Noelle leaned her chin against the heel of her palm—she didn't seem to notice how nervous Lux sounded—and shrugged. "I like to diversify," she said. "Plus, I like faces. And I think portraits look best in black and white."

"Me too," Lux agreed. "The contrasts, right?"

Noelle gave Lux a fraction of a smile. "Yep," she said.

Mr. Van Ness's voice came out of nowhere then, louder than it had been before. "Miss Lee and Miss . . . ?"

"Lawson," Lux supplied, feeling a little embarrassed. He'd been the grumpy, bald teacher she'd interviewed with, so shouldn't he know her name by now?

"Lawson, right. I know you're new, but here at Augusta Savage, we listen to our teachers when they're speaking. So unless you two have something you want to share with the class, can we get back to this chapter on lighting round objects, or do you already know all there is to know about the subject?"

Mr. Van Ness's attitude turned Lux's embarrassment into anger before she could stop it. She hated when grown-ups talked down to her. It reminded her too much of her father.

"I know how to take a good picture." Lux heard the words slip through her lips seconds before she decided they weren't something she should say out loud. She bit the inside of her cheek and slowly added, "Sir."

Noelle raised her eyebrows and shifted in her seat, covering her mouth, probably hiding a grin.

Mr. Van Ness squinted at her. "Oh, really?" he asked, and Lux nodded.

Mr. Van Ness smirked and crossed his arms. "Okay, then," he said, and Lux could tell she'd rubbed him the wrong way. "Then how about you answer a few questions." Lux swallowed hard.

"In low lighting, what ISO setting should you use?" he asked.

"Um . . ." Lux looked around the room as if the answer might appear on a wall. "I'm not sure."

"Name three medium-format film sizes."

"Uh, 220 is one. And, um—" She glanced at Emmett. He wrinkled his brow. He was clearly concerned, but he couldn't just call out the answer to her if he knew it. She started to sweat.

Mr. Van Ness stepped closer to Lux's desk. He towered over her. "If I set my f-stop to f1.8 and my shutter speed to 1/125 of a second . . ." Lux was so mad, she couldn't even hear him anymore.

Her nostrils flared, but she stayed silent.

Mr. Van Ness kept going, and Lux felt her throat ache, the beginning of a rage-cry. She didn't know any of the answers.

She wanted to say, *You don't need to know that stuff to take a good picture*, but she knew she'd already said too much. She'd only just gotten here. How could she be messing things up so soon?

"I don't know," she said. The confession made her skin burn. She couldn't stand giving in. The rest of the class stayed quiet until Emmett raised his hand.

"Exactly, Miss Lawson. You—Yes, Mr. Ortiz?"

"Can you explain when to use the lens on page 150?"

Mr. Van Ness took one final look at Lux that seemed to say *Listen up*, but he answered Emmett's question and left her alone for the rest of the period. Lux still wanted to punch something, or maybe disappear, but then Noelle passed her a tiny, folded note.

Van Ness is a dick. Don't sweat it.

And damn, girl. It took balls to say what you said.

Lux tucked the scrap of paper into her pocket and grinned.

With a bit of asking around, Lux found out when the members of the newspaper met, and later that morning, she swung by to speak to the adviser, Ms. Reddy, about the kinds of photos she liked to take. She brought her photo album. It had felt a bit like a good-luck charm since it helped her get through the admissions interview.

"I think if we took some photos of the fine-arts students in this style, it might make the articles more interesting," Lux explained. "In the last issue, readers could *see* the performing-arts kids. I think the paper should do that for fine arts, too."

Ms. Reddy nodded along as Lux spoke, and she seemed to agree with her. "I never noticed that before, but I see what you mean." Ms. Reddy had light brown skin the color of wet sand, and silky-looking black hair. Lux wanted to take her photo, but she settled on appreciating her bright white smile.

"I think that some documentary-style photography would be nice to go along with the articles, too—images of the visual-arts students actually making the pieces they end up showing." Ms. Reddy nodded, so Lux kept talking. "I could go to the studios, maybe just pick one student for now, while they're working. I'd be quiet, and I'd stay out of their way, I promise. What do you think?"

"I like your initiative, Lux. Why don't we do this . . ." Ms. Reddy flipped another page in Lux's album, looking through it and handing her an assignment for the next edition of the paper all at once. "Let's divide and conquer. I'll have the other student photographer cover the upcoming dance recital. And, Lux, you'll go to the next art show and take the photos in the way you describe *and* the way we've always done them. Bring both sets of photos into the next meeting and we'll all decide as a group which we like better. How's that sound?"

Lux grinned, but she worried the current photographer, whoever they were, would hate her for wanting to get involved with the paper. She remembered how Simone had flipped about her joining double Dutch.

"As for the documentary-style process photos, why don't you shadow Emmett Ortiz? Since you like black-and-white photography, I think his drawings would work well with your style. If it turns out the way I hope, maybe this can become a regular feature—profiling a student and highlighting their work."

Lux sighed. The universe seemed intent on bringing her and this boy together.

"Sounds perfect, Ms. Reddy. Thank you so much for the opportunity."

8

The Yard, where all the students at Savage ate lunch, had picnic tables everywhere and AstroTurf covering the ground. People were sitting on the fake grass, the concrete planters, the tabletops. When Lux got there after her run-in with Van Ness and her meeting with Ms. Reddy, she grabbed a slice of cheese pizza and headed through the sliding glass door that led to the table where she'd spotted Noelle, Tobyn, and Micah. It looked like Tobyn was showing Micah some kind of dance move that she couldn't get right. Noelle laughed and said,

"How's she supposed to do it with no music?" So Tobyn started singing.

"Hey," Lux said. "Sorry to interrupt." She hadn't had the nerve to sit with them over the last couple of weeks, but after Noelle's note, she felt bold enough to try. "What are you guys doing?"

Tobyn stopped singing and rolled her eyes. "Ugh, nothing. Micah just isn't musically gifted. I don't know why I even try."

Micah rolled her eyes then. "I have other talents," she said to Lux, and she pointed to an empty spot at the picnic table. "Sit with us!" she insisted.

Lux hesitated and glanced at Noelle, who squealed, "You guys will not believe what *she* said to Van Ness this morning." That was all Lux needed. She sat and blushed as Noelle told the story, clearly impressed with her. Lux's embarrassment about the exchange morphed into pride.

"Damn, girl!" Micah said.

"I know, right?" Tobyn agreed. "Didn't know you had it in you."

Lux shrugged, secretly pleased to have done something that surprised them. She noticed a copy of the school paper on the table and wanted to tell them about her assignment, but when she glanced at the list of staff, she saw something that made her freeze.

NOELLE LEE . . . . PHOTOGRAPHER

Oh no, Lux thought.

"So, Lux. We've been dying to know. Why'd you transfer in the middle of the year?" Noelle asked, breaking Lux's concentration. "And what *I* really want to know is how the hell you got in."

Tobyn leaned forward on the bench. "Not

gonna lie, I've been wondering the same thing. I remember auditioning when I was like fourteen. Kids left crying. And you just get in as a junior? Do you, like, know someone?"

Lux knew this moment would come—that they'd want to know her history. "My mom pulled some strings," Lux said, repeating the words her dad used. She really didn't know how she'd gotten in. And she didn't want to answer Noelle's first question—about why she needed to be there in the first place. But Noelle didn't stop watching her closely. She wasn't going to let Lux get away with keeping any secrets.

Luckily, the bell rang, and Lux had never been more grateful for that annoying, shrill sound. They all stood to head back to class, but Micah hung back.

"If you're worried about Van Ness," Micah

said, "I can show you all that stuff he tried to embarrass you about—the lenses and lights or whatever. I mean, if you want."

Lux blinked. "Really?"

"Sure."

"How do you know so much about it?"

"Well," Micah said, "even though I'm focusing on fine arts, I signed up for photography classes as electives because I like to include photos in my pieces. Plus, a lot of the color, light, and theory stuff they teach you guys applies to painting and drawing, too. *And* a lot of the fine-arts kids are weirdos—I say that with love— so a daily break from them is needed."

Lux grinned. "Thanks," she said.

"No problem. I can't do today because I gotta go to a prayer service with my parents." Micah sighed. "Such is the life of a church girl." Lux remembered that Micah's parents were

Christian and made church into a really big deal for the whole family. "But wait for us after school, maybe on Wednesday? You can just come over."

As Lux sat through the rest of her classes, she wondered if joining the paper was worth risking Noelle's (and the other girls') friendship. But after the run-in that morning with Mr. Van Ness, Lux knew she needed something to keep the simmering rage inside her quiet.

❧

"I saw you hanging around with Tobyn Wolfe and Micah Dupree," Emmett said to her in the hall that afternoon. She'd been doing everything she could to avoid him, but she couldn't duck him before and after school because their lockers were so close together.

"Yeah, so?" she said.

"I'm wondering if you know what you're getting into, being friends with them and Noelle Lee."

Lux laughed. "Getting into? I didn't know you'd be so concerned with who I'm friends with, *Dad*." she said to him.

"Ha, ha, ha," he said sarcastically. "It's just that the Flyy Girls are like the queens of the junior class."

"The Flyy Girls?" Lux asked.

"Yeah. See? You *don't* know what you're getting into. Everybody calls them the Flyy Girls because they fly under the radar. They do all this crazy stuff, but they never get caught. When we were freshmen, they released butterflies in the halls—like hundreds of them. Last year, they all wore butterfly wings to the spring formal, kinda admitting it so that everyone knew it was them. But no one had any proof, so nothing happened."

Lux grinned. She hadn't expected this.

"And, I don't know," Emmett continued. "You don't seem like them."

Lux could imagine it: the three of them walking into that dance like they owned the place. She wished she had been there to take a photo of that. She wished she had been there beside them with her own set of wings fanning out behind her.

"Flyy Girls," Lux said to herself, and then said to Emmett, "I might not seem like them, but I don't really seem like anyone."

"Exactly," Emmett replied, "That's what I like about you."

But he didn't get it.

That was the problem she was always trying to fix.

That night, Lux had dinner with her father. She'd been pretty busy trying to stay on top of her homework, and she often went to a coffee shop or the library after school to study instead of heading back to the noisy apartment. Lillia's crying wasn't exactly great for focusing. But Luke told her he'd made reservations, so she was happy to have her dad all to herself.

The two of them sat in a Mexican place a few blocks from their building, and it felt like one of the too-short visits they'd had last year. She tried not to think about how depressing those visits had been, though, because at least he seemed to be trying now. When her father asked her about her first few weeks of school, she told him almost everything.

"It's a really cool place," Lux said, putting

down her fork for a minute. "I mean, you saw how the hallways were painted when we went in for my interview—all those colors? But that's just the beginning. There's this courtyard where everyone eats lunch. Everyone calls it the Yard, and it's way better than any school cafeteria."

"A courtyard, in the beginning of March?" her father asked.

"Well, it's enclosed. Kinda like a greenhouse?"

"Ah, I see."

"Yeah. And I met a few cool people, too," she said before taking a big bite of her tamale. "There's this girl named Tobyn who is at Savage for singing. Sometimes she just sings in the middle of the hallways. She's always dancing, too, and I think she could do either if she wanted. She has an older sister who is in this band, and they have gigs all over the city."

"Wow. That's pretty impressive. Did her

sister go to Savage, too?"

"She did, a few years ago, I think. And then there's this girl named Micah who's there for visual arts. She's really sweet. And Noelle is there for cello, but she also takes a lot of classes in other subjects and is in a million extracurriculars because she's, like, such an overachiever."

"See, Luxana? These are the sorts of people you should have been surrounding yourself with this whole time. I knew if you just made the right kinds of friends and got your priorities in order, you could turn things around." Her father looked proud and it made her chest swell. She decided not to mention that her new friends were also epic pranksters. "How are your classes?" he asked next.

She described how the classrooms were all painted a different bright color, just like the hallways, and how she liked most of her teachers. It made her feel light, talking to him the way she would have spoken to her mom. She thought that maybe moving in with him was a better idea than it initially seemed.

He smiled and said, "Your teachers seem impressed with you. And I heard you've shown some interest in joining the school paper." Lux nodded at first, but then she frowned at him and stopped chewing.

"Wait. How do you know that?" she asked.

"I checked in."

"With who?" Lux asked, setting her fork on the edge of her plate.

"With your teachers. I just made a few phone calls. Oh, don't look at me like that, Lux. I told you things would be different now that you're living with me. And it's obviously working—having a bit more structure. You seem to be doing remarkably well."

Lux didn't know why his checking in on her made her angry, but she could feel the back of her neck getting hot. He didn't trust her. And in that moment, their pleasant evening fell away, and she remembered all at once why she couldn't trust him, either.

She'd never forget the morning she woke up to find him and all of his things gone. It had been so sudden that she'd wondered if he'd died.

"Where's Dad?" she asked Genevieve in a panic.

Her mother sat in their kitchen, sipping a cup of coffee. "Oh, honey," her mother said. She turned to Lux with tears in her eyes, and Lux understood instantly that her mother's sadness had more to do with Lux's surprise than her own. "This has been a long time coming. He's gone, but we're going to be fine."

Lux tore her room apart looking for a note from him. An explanation of where he'd gone and why. But she didn't find one.

"Did he leave anything?" she asked her mother later. "Like, anything for me?"

Genevieve looked at her daughter. "I told him if he didn't have the guts to stay and face you, he better not leave anything behind for you to find."

Lux hated Genevieve for that for a long time. Until she realized that her father chose to go rather than wait a few hours for her to wake up. And when she'd asked him to explain himself, and told him a note would have been better than nothing at all, he could only say, "Your mother thought this would be best."

He'd left her once without so much as a goodbye, and so it felt easy to imagine him disappearing from her life again if she didn't live up to his expectations.

Now, Lux wanted to throw salsa at him and storm out—she wanted to be the one who left. "I wish you hadn't called my teachers," Lux said softly.

Her father pressed his lips together. "Honey, I'm just trying to set you up for success. When you have kids of your own, you'll understand." Lux hated when he dismissed her like that, but she suffered her way through the rest of the meal, and when they got home, she went to her room and didn't come back out.

—march 10—

I'm still at Dad's.

I guess it's getting a little bit better. I called mom tonight and told her about the first few weeks of school, she seemed happy for me. Maybe I'll really get to move back in with her soon if I stay out of trouble.

If I do move, I hope I get to keep going to Savage. Even though I hate mr. Van Ness with every inch of my body, everyone else is pretty cool, especially micah, Tobyn, and Noelle.

Yesterday, Emmett said I don't seem like them . . . I'm not sure what that means, but I think I kinda want to be like them. Or at least fit in with them.

Speaking of Emmett . . . I'm photographing him for the paper, and even though I've been trying to keep my distance from boys, this assignment is making that . . . difficult.

I spent an hour in the studio with him today, taking pictures of his charcoal sketches and watching him smear the black lines he drew into hair and cheekbones and dark eyes. He asked to draw me, but that would be waaaay too embarrassing.

This would all be fine—taking his picture and having classes with him and even his flirting— if he wasn't so damn cute! And he's nice, too. He helped distract Van Ness the last time he was laying into me. It's impossible to ignore him, as much as I want to.

I'm going to Micah's tomorrow, and I'm really nervous. It's the first time I'm hanging out with the "Flyy Girls" outside of school. I hope I don't screw this up.

9

Lux texted her dad while she waited for Micah and her friends the next day. *Going to a friend's house after school,* she sent, and after he'd replied telling her to be home by "nineteen hundred"—seven o'clock—she stared at one of the words: *friend.* She didn't know if Noelle, Tobyn, and Micah would consider her a friend the way she'd already started thinking of them, but the possibility made her insides ache a little.

She felt jittery and nervous, so she took out her camera and started snapping pictures of everything while she waited for them. She turned to take a photo of the mural on the doors of the school, and to her surprise, a boy stepped in front of her camera.

"Hi," Emmett said.

"Hey," Lux said. "It's you. But you're wearing glasses."

He grinned and straightened the pair of wiry frames like he was a little self-conscious of them. "It is me. And yeah, I only use them for distance . . . like in class when I'm sitting in the back. Or . . . to see if the cute girl standing on the stairs is the same one who took pictures of me."

Lux squinted at him. Emmett looked like he might be blushing, but his dark skin couldn't show it. This pushed him from the *Kinda Cute* box in Lux's head to the *Downright Adorable* one. He cleared his throat.

"Waiting for someone?" Emmett asked.

"Yeah. But not you," Lux said. She smiled to soften the words as they landed. She'd stopped herself from flirting yesterday afternoon when they shared the small studio space, but now that they were in the open air, she couldn't help it.

Emmett smirked. "Right. But if I asked you to take another photo of me, would you?"

He leaned against the brick wall of the building. He tilted his head up to the sun and closed his eyes.

Lux laughed, and he lifted one eyebrow. He said, "That was easier than I thought."

"What was?" Lux asked.

"Getting you to laugh."

Emmett swallowed nervously and Lux watched his Adam's apple scoot up and down his neck. Lux would love to have a boy like this:

a soft and sweet boy who said nice things to her just because he'd thought them. But she couldn't risk it. She'd do something wrong, the way she always did, and ruin everything. Or worse, he'd let her down and she'd never forgive him.

Lux looked down at her camera and scrolled past the few photos she'd just snapped of Emmett. "I should actually go," she said. She'd wait for Micah, Tobyn, and Noelle on the train station platform if she had to.

"Cool," Emmett said, grinning. "Me too. See you tomorrow, Lux."

Lux watched him walk away, and then she left in the opposite direction.

※

On the subway with Micah, Noelle, and

Tobyn, Lux felt a little . . . lost. She could navigate the train system with her eyes closed, but finding her way into a conversation with these girls was another story.

"Did you see Ms. Taylor's socks today?" Noelle said to Micah.

"Oh my God, no," Micah answered, making a face as Noelle handed over her phone. Micah laughed at whatever played on the screen. Then she pulled her own phone out. "But did you hear about Tamera and Jason?"

"Noelle," Tobyn cut in, pulling out one of her earbuds. She'd been humming to herself like the other girls weren't even there. "You *have* to hear this song."

If they weren't underground, Lux would have just stared out the window and waited for the ride to be over. But she had nothing to look at down here but dark tunnel walls and other trains passing them on the opposite track.

"Micah," Noelle said, "are your parents gonna be home?"

"Doubt it," Micah said, then she finally turned to address Lux. "We can only go up to the roof when they're gone," Micah explained. "My mom's weird about the roof. But Noelle loves it up there."

When Micah grabbed Lux's hand and asked if she could borrow the gold nail polish, she nodded and relaxed her fingers a little. She hadn't noticed how tightly she'd been clutching her phone.

∗⋈∗

They stopped inside Micah's apartment for only a moment. It was smaller than Lux's father's apartment, but bigger than the one she'd shared with her mom. She, Tobyn, and Noelle leaned against the walls in the front hallway while Micah made hot chocolate for everyone and grabbed her photography stuff. They didn't even take their coats off. As soon as the mugs were in their hands, they went to the roof.

"It's the golden hour," Micah said to Lux. "Know what that is?"

Lux looked out over the edge of the building at the city skyline. She had heard that term before and knew it had something to do with sunset; something to do with the quality of this exact light and how it's perfect for taking a gorgeous photo.

"Kinda," Lux said. "That's actually the name of this color." She wiggled her fingers so they could see her nails again.

"Really?" Micah asked. Lux nodded, sipped

her cocoa, and turned to look at the other girls. "That's why we had to get up here fast. Okay, so," Micah said. She pulled out different lenses and quickly explained each one as she fitted them onto her camera and handed it to Lux so she could look through to see the subtle but important differences. Noelle and Tobyn were sipping their drinks and lounging on a few rusty chairs that someone had left up on the roof. Lux aimed the camera at them and snapped.

The girls talked until the golden light sank toward darkness. Tobyn talked about her girlfriend, Ava. "I can't believe she wants to go see my sister's band. They suck, so you know she must really love me," she said. They all laughed.

Micah talked about her boyfriend, Ty, and her newest art piece. "It's gonna just be different parks around New York. Focusing on the green in the city instead of all the gray. But I'm thinking about shooting it in black and white, and then painting buildings made of leaves? It's kinda hard to explain. You guys will just have to wait and see it."

Noelle talked about her grandparents' restaurant in Chinatown and how she had to work there after school tomorrow. Lux looked at her a little more closely now. Noelle had dark skin and wild, curly hair, but Lux could see other, minor features in her face, too—hints at the fact that her father was Chinese American.

Lux mostly stayed quiet, afraid of giving too much of herself away too early. But she did say, "Is it true you guys released butterflies in the halls freshman year?"

Noelle nodded, smirking.

Tobyn said, "How'd you know?"

Micah said, "God, it was beautiful. And we made sure the windows were open so they just flew straight through." Lux laughed and snapped photos of them as they talked, then moved around the roof, taking pictures of the view.

"Sophomore year, we hid cheap alarm clocks in every classroom. Like, *really* hid them. And set them all to go off at the same time," Noelle said.

"We got early dismissal because none of the teachers could find the clocks and disable the alarms," Tobyn added. "It was epic."

"You guys do this every year?" Lux asked, and they all nodded. "Damn."

"So, you never really told us why you had to change schools in the middle of the year," Noelle brought up again. Lux swallowed hard and lowered her camera.

"I just had to move in with my dad," Lux said. "My parents split up," she continued, and she hoped that would be enough.

"That sucks," Micah said. "Sorry."

Lux shrugged. "It's whatever."

As Tobyn changed the subject and Micah went back to her photography book, Noelle still watched Lux. It looked like she didn't believe a word Lux had said.

10

Instead of heading home right away, Lux hopped on the train back to her old neighborhood. The art show was coming up, and after trying out the techniques Micah had shown her on the roof, she wanted to look through the camera lenses and stuff she'd left behind in her bedroom to see if she'd need any of them. She also wanted to see her mom. But when she got off at the stop closest to her old apartment, she spotted a group of girls from her old school hanging out on the platform.

Ignoring them would be easy enough, she

thought, but then she noticed Bree and a few of Simone's other friends in the group. Her heart sped up instantly, and her mouth went dry.

"Luxana Lawson."

Bree had spotted her, and she said Lux's name like it was a curse word. All the other girls turned to look and started heading toward her.

None of them had done a thing during the fight at school besides pull up the cameras on their phones, but now, all at once, they seemed set on hurting her just like she'd hurt Simone. Lux wondered if they hung back at school because they'd actually read the student handbook and knew they'd get expelled for fighting. Now that she thought about it, maybe Simone pissed her off on purpose, hoping Lux would get angry enough to hit her first. Simone's whole plan could have been to get her kicked out of school so she could have her precious spot on the double Dutch team. The thought made Lux hot with rage, but even she knew she couldn't fight all seven of the girls who were coming her way.

"'Scuse me. Sorry. MOVE!" She pushed past and through everyone around her. It was rush hour, which helped and hurt Lux—it kept the girls from catching up with her too quickly, but it slowed down her progress, too.

She made it to the lower platform and ducked behind a trash can a few feet away from the stairs. A train pulled in just as she started to pray for one. The girls' loud voices bounced off the walls of the stairwell as they moved toward her.

Lux chanced a glance around the trash can before flipping up the hood of her jacket and rushing onto the train the second the doors opened.

Lux didn't let herself breathe until she heard the doors of the train close. Through the subway window, she saw the girls exit the stairway and stumble onto the platform—just a minute too late.

The train and Lux were going in the exact opposite direction of her dad's apartment. She'd be cutting it close to her seven o'clock curfew, and she hadn't even gotten to see her mom. But at least she didn't get jumped.

"If you can't make it back here by curfew," Luke said when Lux walked in at 7:02 p.m., "you'll lose the privilege to go *anywhere* after school."

He was feeding Lillia, and the infant sucked at the bottle like her life depended on it.

Her father didn't even look up at Lux as he spoke—he kept his eyes on the baby. Lux double-checked the time, and yep, she'd gotten in as close to seven as she'd thought she did. She'd even run part of the way home.

"You serious?" Lux said. Tired both from the long day at school and from being chased, Lux started to feel like nothing she did would ever be good enough for her father.

"I am very serious," he said. He finally looked away from his four-week-old baby and up at his seventeen-year-old daughter. "Don't let it happen again. I also checked in with some of your teachers this week and I got a bad report from one of them. I'm not happy, Luxana."

Lux rolled her eyes (she knew it had to have been Van Ness), and her father put the bottle down. He stood up and stepped closer to her so quickly that Lux took a step backward.

"Don't let *that*"—he pointed to her rolling eyes— "happen again, either. And you need to get your priorities straight at school, or your mother and I will have to . . . reconsider . . . what the plan will be for you next year."

He didn't say *military school*, but Lux knew that was what he meant. She wanted to tell him she didn't care, that he could send her wherever he wanted. But before their fight got any worse, another voice entered their conversation.

"Luke," Penny said. She sounded sleepy as she stepped into the kitchen, but her eyes looked serious. "We talked about this. Lux is doing well. Let's maybe not jeopardize that with threats?" Penny looked at Lux and smiled. Her father handed Lillia to Penny and sat back down. She wished he'd decided to back off on his own, but she didn't hate the feeling of someone in this apartment being on her side. "Why don't you head to your room?" Penny said to Lux. "I'm sure you have some homework to do before dinner."

Lux looked down at Lillia instead of at her father. The kid got even cuter when she wasn't screaming. "We both got lucky with pretty cool moms, huh, kid?" she whispered. Lillia cooed, and Lux glanced up at Penny. "Thanks," she said before going to her room.

❦

After finishing her homework, Lux checked her phone. She was surprised to see a message from Danika. It read, *Have you seen this?*

Lux clicked the link and saw another video. It had to have been recorded a few weeks ago, because in it, Simone still had two black eyes and a bandaged nose. Her bruises were fading, but as Lux looked at the damage she'd caused, it made her stomach drop.

"You see this?" Simone said into the camera. She leaned closer, showing off the bruised and swollen parts of her face. "My parents are thinking about pressing charges, but we haven't decided yet. We have all the proof we need: pictures, medical bills, and eyewitnesses. But they don't know if it's worth the money to go to court. I think it is. I mean, I could have been a *model* before this, and now—"

Lux swiped the video away. She didn't bother messaging Danika back.

Her dad might have known she'd gotten into a fight, but she didn't need him (or anyone else) to be able to *see* exactly what she'd done. And the threat of a lawsuit made Lux feel faint. He already didn't trust her, so she knew Luke wouldn't listen if she told him what really happened with Simone. He cared more about how things looked than the truth. And this looked *bad*.

If her parents found out about the videos, it might be enough to convince them that she should have gone to military school after all.

The next week, Lux still felt antsy after seeing Simone's video, but when Noelle said hi to her first thing Monday morning, some small part of her relaxed. She'd been eating lunch with the girls every day now, and she almost felt like she could be her real, complete self around them. She tried to focus on how well things were going instead of her one constant worry: that they'd find her out.

"So I think," Noelle said, walking with Lux down the long main hall of the school, "you could use some noodles."

Lux frowned at her. "Noodles?" she asked.

"Noodles," Noelle said. "And also maybe some dumplings. Perhaps an egg roll to round it out, and an egg tart for dessert?"

"What are you talking about, Noelle?"

Noelle stopped her from walking. "I know you always go to the library after school."

"Oh yeah. My dad's wife just had a new baby and she cries a lot. Libraries are quiet."

"Right, but libraries don't have delicious Chinese food. My grandparents' restaurant, on the other hand . . ."

"You're inviting me to your grandparents' restaurant?" Lux asked. Noelle nodded. "Why?"

"Oh my God, do you think I'm going to murder you or something? Are you going to come or not? Tobyn and Micah will be there, too, but I'm not going to beg."

Lux squinted at Noelle like she could see

through to her motives if she looked at her hard enough. Maybe she did just want to hang out. Lux wasn't sure how she should feel, but she reminded herself that she wanted this.

"Okay," Lux said.

"Cool." Noelle smiled. "The girls will be happy you're coming."

◆※◆

Noelle's grandparents' restaurant was squeezed between two apartment buildings. So many signs and menus covered the glass door so that you couldn't see inside.

Noelle had asked Lux to come by but hadn't said why, and as the day went on, Lux began to worry it might be about the newspaper— that she'd found out Lux wanted to become a member of the staff and planned to confront her about trying to take her position.

Lux slipped inside and sat at a table near the front windows. She didn't see Micah or Tobyn anywhere, but she had gotten there early. Before she'd even taken her backpack all the way off, Noelle appeared wearing a green T-shirt that said **LEE'S DUMPLINGS**. Lux looked around the restaurant and saw a few young white couples eating and a half dozen older Chinese customers, too. They were the only black girls, and Lux felt completely out of place. She wondered if Noelle ever felt that way, even though she was half Chinese.

Lux said, "Hey," but Noelle didn't.

"So, I'll be honest with you. Micah and Tobyn aren't coming."

"Okay . . ." Lux squirmed in her seat and glanced around the half-empty restaurant again. "So why am I here?"

"My friends like you," Noelle said. "And before we tell you about the next prank we're planning, I need to know we can trust you."

So this *was* gonna be about the paper, then. "Look, Noelle," Lux started to say, "I wanted to tell you—" But Noelle pulled out her phone and cut Lux off.

"Is this you?" she asked. She held out her phone, and on the screen, Lux saw a video of her fighting Simone. It showed a different angle from the one she'd untagged last month. Her twists swung from side to side, but even from this angle, her face thankfully remained hidden. She frowned.

"I'm sorry, what?" Lux said. "You think I'd risk messing up my hair, or more importantly, *my nails*, fighting?" She must have pulled off looking completely confused, because Noelle laughed.

"I had a feeling it wasn't you." Noelle pocketed her phone, looking relieved. "It's just that I saw it a while ago, and the girl who posted it goes to your old school in Brooklyn. The hair looks exactly like yours and you'd just shown up out of nowhere. I don't know. I had to ask because we can't risk this kind of sloppiness with the stuff we do. A video that got posted? Can't happen. My parents would kill me if they ever found out about the stunts we pull."

Lux smiled uncomfortably. "I get it," she said. "My dad would flip, too."

"So we cool?" Noelle asked. "Yeah," Lux said. "We're good."

Noelle left the table and came back with a dozen dumplings, a heaping plate of noodles, and that egg tart she mentioned, but Lux didn't have an appetite at all. She choked a bit of it down, then begged for a take-out box.

"My dad loves Chinese food," she said.

Noelle grinned. "I mean, who doesn't?"

But as Lux said goodbye and headed home, her mind wouldn't stop spinning. If Noelle had seen that video, Lux worried it would only be a matter of time before she found the other ones.

At the art show, Lux couldn't stop looking at Micah's piece.

She took dozens of photos of it. Micah had made a collage that incorporated black-and-white shots taken in parks all over the city, just like she'd described: the tops of trees, the reservoir in Central Park, the view from the top of the stairs of the biggest park in Fort Greene. Around and behind them, Micah had painted lush greenery, bright flowers, and blue sky in the shapes of buildings.

Lux then moved around the rest of the

show, taking photo after photo of sculptures, sketches, paintings, collages, light installations, and the kids who made them. There were even a few multimedia pieces with flashing laptops or monitors.

She was actually having fun, and when Tobyn and Noelle arrived, the show got even better. Noelle seemed to be watching Lux closely, but then she came over and started asking Lux if she needed help.

"I do," Lux said, and without hesitation, Noelle started art directing. She told one fine-arts student to tilt his head a little more toward the light, and another one to kneel next to her creation. She'd look at the display on Lux's camera to decide if she liked the shot and ask Lux what she thought, too. It felt a little bossy, but Lux knew by now that that was just Noelle. Tobyn laughed the whole time.

Lux couldn't decide how to tell Noelle that these photos were for an assignment from Ms. Reddy for the paper. She started and stopped half a dozen times, but every time she got close to saying the words *I'm taking photos for the paper,* she got too afraid of what Noelle might think or say or do.

At the end of the long exhibit hall, Lux found Emmett standing next to a series of his sketches. One showed a pair of clasped hands, another had two different ears sharing a set of earbuds, and a final one featured a girl's long braids tangled in another person's Afro. The series, according to a little paper sign next to him on the wall, was titled *Closer.* Lux swallowed hard as she clicked her camera and moved closer, like the sign read.

"Hey," she said. And she thought this might be the first time she ever spoke to him first.

"Hi," he said. "Where do you want me?"

He must have been watching as Noelle walked with her around the show floor, telling people where to stand, how to move. But now Noelle stood over by Tobyn and Micah, talking.

"I don't direct," Lux said. "Just act natural." He had his glasses on, and it made the pit of her stomach feel heavy when he reached up to straighten them. She clicked her camera more.

"I remember someone who looked a lot like you telling me not to smile on your first day here."

Lux smirked. "Touché," she said. "Tell me more about your sketches."

He turned and looked at the wall like he'd forgotten why he was there. "It's not that deep. It's just about first love. The way it catches you by surprise. The way all you want is to be closer to that one person."

Lux lowered her camera and stepped up to the wall. "The finished products are gorgeous," she said, and she meant it.

"Thanks," Emmett replied, and his voice sounded close.

Lux turned around to see him standing right behind her. She hadn't registered that he was so much taller than her, broad and big, but with gentle eyes.

She cleared her throat and took a step away from him. She lifted her camera and captured the way he looked at her. She'd probably keep that photo for herself.

It was getting harder and harder to keep her distance from Emmett Ortiz.

A second later, he looked around her and squinted.

"Is that Ms. Reddy?" Emmett asked.

It was. Lux had the photos she needed,

and she couldn't wait to show them off to her, but she'd planned to bring them to the next newspaper staff meeting. She turned around to look for Noelle. But she was with Ms. Reddy, and the two were walking in Lux's direction.

"I'm gonna go," Lux told Emmett. The sight of her teacher and her new friend walking toward her filled her belly with dread.

He grinned. "Thanks for the pictures," he said.

Ms. Reddy and Noelle reached Lux before she could leave the room, and she heard Noelle say, "The girl's got skills. You were totally right to assign her to this show."

Lux turned around to look at them. "You knew?" she asked, surprised.

"Of course I knew!" Noelle said. "Ms. Reddy told us at the last staff meeting that we had a new student interested in helping out with the 'photographic direction' of the paper. I had a feeling it was you."

Ms. Reddy grinned. "I'm so glad you two are getting along! I asked Noelle to give you a few pointers, though I could tell from your album and our last conversation how much natural talent and vision you have for this kind of work."

"Oh," Lux said. She let out a breathy laugh. "I was so nervous to tell you!" she said to Noelle. "I thought you'd think I wanted to steal your spot or something."

Noelle shrugged. "Nah. It would be worse to share the job with someone who sucks. But you're cool."

—April 12—

It's spring break and I'm spending the whole week at Mom's, making sure I steer clear of kids from my old school.

Last night, me and the girls went to see Tobyn's sister's band play a show. The band is called Boys Behaving Badly, even though all five members are girls. Tobyn's sister Devyn sings, and Tobyn was right when she said they sucked—her sister is really the only talented one.

Tobyn's girlfriend, Ava, came with us, and Micah invited her boyfriend, Ty. Noelle brought her boyfriend, Travis . . . and also invited Emmett, even though I asked her not to.

No one called it a date, but at one point

during the night, everyone paired off. Tobyn and Ava went to grab a soda, and Micah and Ty started kissing. Noelle pulled Travis up to the stage so they'd be closer to the music, and me and Emmett were left in the middle of the crowd alone.

He asked how my studio photos were going, and I showed him a few I had saved on my phone. And when the band started playing again, he put his arms around my hips, and I didn't move away when he started dancing with me.

Finding Emmett wasn't a part of the plan, but I'm so happy to have people I care about again.

The night ended with all of us up on Micah's roof. Tobyn and her sister sang whatever song we requested. Noelle pointed out different buildings in the skyline. I showed

Micah how I did my twists, and she put a few in Ava's hair. I watched while the boys played cards. I think I forgot what having real friends feels like.

13

Her first night back at her dad's after break, Lux walked into the apartment well before curfew but didn't see anyone at home. She'd expected her father to be waiting up for her, since she'd been away all week, but he wasn't in the kitchen or the living room. Maybe he and Penny had dropped Lillia off at a neighbor's apartment and gone out for dinner.

Lux counted herself lucky to have the whole place to herself and sat down on the couch to scroll through all the photos she'd taken over break. There were shots from Micah's roof and a ton from the Boys Behaving Badly show. She picked out a few of her favorites and started editing them on her laptop.

She video-called Noelle for help with the editing software she'd just gotten, but as soon as Noelle picked up, she heard a bedroom door shut softly. And then her father appeared, and Penny stood right behind him. The second he saw her, his whole face twisted in anger.

"I'll call you back," Lux said before Noelle even said hello. She tossed her phone and it landed near one of the throw pillows seconds before her father spoke.

"You *broke* a girl's *nose*?" he whispered fiercely. "And now her parents want to press charges?"

Lux had seen her father annoyed. She'd seen him tired. She'd even seen him happy, or as close to happiness as he let himself show.

But she'd never seen him this angry in her entire life.

Lux was so surprised that she didn't say anything right away. She looked desperately in Penny's direction, but she didn't come to her rescue this time. Lux hadn't heard or seen anything about the potential lawsuit in weeks, but somehow he'd found out about Simone's threats.

"It was an accident," Lux finally whispered back.

"You're grounded. You're doing nothing but homework, school, and meals with Penny and me for the foreseeable future. I don't understand why you do things like this. A fight is one thing, but breaking a girl's nose and potentially getting involved in a lawsuit? You've been kicked out of three schools in the last year for fighting. I'd finally gotten over that, but now there's this video? I thought you were doing so well. I just don't understand where your mom and I went wrong. Why can't you just be a good kid?"

Lux could hear him whispering that last question again as he walked away, but it felt louder than if he had yelled. His eyes looked so disappointed, even though his words made it sound like he'd expected something like this from her all along.

Lux felt it swirling, whatever *it* was that so often went wild inside her. She followed her dad into the kitchen and saw Penny heating up a bottle for Lillia; she looked at the black-and-white newborn portraits hanging on the wall, at his and Penny's wedding photos. There were no photos of her here, like she didn't even exist.

And just like that, her mind took her back to her old apartment on the day he left, waking up and discovering him and everything he owned gone. Tearing apart her room, looking for a note from him that she would never find. She didn't understand then, but maybe him leaving without saying goodbye was the reason behind every mood swing she'd had in the last year. He left her and he didn't even care until she'd gotten into enough fights that military school seemed like the only solution.

Lux looked at her father and replayed all the ways he'd made her feel like she wasn't enough. It made her want to destroy everything around her.

"Why can't I just be a good kid?" she shouted. "Maybe because you left me!" Penny dropped the bottle in her hand. From the other room, Lillia started crying, but Lux didn't care.

"Maybe because you love Penny and Lillia more than you love me! Maybe because you make me feel like crap all the time! Did any of that occur to you, *Daddy*?"

She hadn't said *Daddy* since she'd moved in, and she hadn't realized it until that moment.

Her father's eyes went glassy, but Lux knew he wasn't sad, just angry. Penny had to lead him back to their room. Lux realized then that her mother had been right all the times she'd said Lux got her temper from her father.

"So it *was* you. In that video."

The voice sounded low and seemed to be coming from under a pillow. When she pulled it away, Noelle's face still showed on the screen.

"You told us you came to Savage because your parents split up. But it was because of that fight."

Lux stared at her but didn't know what to say.

"And then you lied to my face about it," Noelle continued.

Lux sat frozen. She couldn't move.

"Wow. Guess it's good to know who you really are."

"I thought I'd hung up," Lux said numbly. Dumbly.

"Yeah, I did too," she said slowly. "I went to the bathroom, but when I came back into my room, I heard voices. I thought my music had turned on at first, but then I realized it was my phone. I heard it all."

"I just wanted to be your friend," Lux finally said.

Noelle frowned. "Real friends don't lie, do they?"

Lux didn't know what to say.

"Bye, Lux," Noelle said, and hung up.

As soon as it sounded like everyone had gone to sleep, Lux packed a bag. She caught the train to her mom's apartment and used her key to let herself in.

"Mommy?" she said quietly, standing at her mother's bedroom door.

"Lux?" her mom answered sleepily. "What are you doing back here?"

"Are you mad at me, too?"

Her mother rubbed her eyes and frowned. "Yes, but we'll deal with that in the morning."

Lux didn't say anything else. She just crawled into bed with her mother. She cried and slept and tried not to dream about how much more trouble she'd be in with her father for leaving. And even though she was mad, Genevieve held her daughter tightly all night long.

The whole next week, Lux's parents were trying to work something out—a schedule where Lux would be able to see her mom more often, at least on the weekends—but Genevieve agreed to let Lux stay with her until the end of the week. She had to come straight home from school after doing her homework in the library, and she had to show her mom every assignment she finished. But she got to sleep in her own bed. So far, she hadn't run into Bree or any of Simone's other friends, but she'd been leaving for school early to avoid them and coming home late, too.

Lux wasn't sure what would happen with Simone. Her mother told her about the call from Mr. Harding, Simone's father, and how he'd said they were "weighing their options." She told Lux that she couldn't afford a lawyer and so it would fall to Luke to hire one if it came to that. Lux told her mom about the bullying, about the way Simone's friends had been tagging her online, and about the time they'd chased her, and her mom said, "That could help us if this goes any further. I wished you'd told me about that sooner."

School hadn't been much better. The girls kept their distance from her. She'd gone to Micah's rooftop with them nearly every week since that first time, but not anymore.

And in the halls, Noelle, Tobyn, and Micah acted like Lux didn't even exist. So Lux went back to playing that part—the invisible girl. Their friendship had been nice while it lasted, but she should have known it wouldn't be forever.

Of course Mr. Van Ness chose that week to press all of Lux's buttons, so it didn't surprise her that she got into it with him again. This time, their disagreement had to do with framing.

"You can set up a good shot and wait for something interesting to walk into the frame. Sometimes you have to be patient. The shot can come to you," he said.

Lux raised her hand and asked, "But isn't that a little fake? To set something up and wait? I thought photography is more about being in the right place at the right time?"

"Yes, but photography is also an art. And art is often about patience, Luxana. It's like fishing. You go to a spot with possibility, and you wait."

Nothing he said really upset Lux, other than his use of her full name. Up until that point, he'd only referred to her as Miss Lawson. But when he said Luxana, all she could think about was her father.

"My name is Lux," she said, not loudly, but definitely loud enough to be heard, even though Mr. Van Ness had already turned his back to her.

"I'm sorry?" he asked, turning back around. "Did you say something?"

"I said, 'My name is Lux.' Not Luxana. So I'd prefer you call me Lux. Please."

Mr. Van Ness walked back over to his desk and looked at something on the surface. "Looks like your name, according to this, is Luxana Lawson. So your name *is* actually Luxana."

"So you won't mind me calling you Felix, then?" Lux said before she could stop herself.

Around the classroom, kids laughed and covered their mouths. She'd been doing so well. But that landed her in detention.

Lux walked into the part of the school library where they held detention. It was her third day of being stuck there, and she didn't expect to see a familiar face already seated at one of the tables.

"What are you in for?" Lux whispered as she sat down next to Emmett. Someone immediately shushed her and reminded her of the *No talking in the library* rule.

"You know, I shouldn't be talking to you," he said the second the adviser stopped watching them.

Lux smirked. "Because I'm a troublemaker?"

she asked, and Emmett nodded.

"Clearly."

"You're one to talk," she said, pointing to the table where they were sitting and then to the sign on the adviser's desk that read **DETENTION 2:30–3:30 P.M.** in bold letters. "You're in here with me, aren't you?"

"Touché," Emmett said. "The strange thing is, I miss talking to you."

With things still being weird with the girls, and because she was already on very thin ice with her parents, Lux hadn't been hanging around after school or even in between classes. It *had* been a while since they spoke. And he missed her. Lux looked at her notebook so he wouldn't see her smile.

"Did you hear that Ms. Reddy picked three of your photos from the art show to run in the paper this week?" Emmett asked the next time he had a chance to talk to Lux.

"What?" Lux whispered back. She hadn't been to the last staff meeting for the paper because she'd been stuck in detention, and she hadn't asked Noelle about any of it for obvious reasons. She'd emailed her best photos to Ms. Reddy, but she hadn't heard back from her.

"Yeah," Emmett said. "I only know because she picked one of me and I had to give my permission for it to run. You're good, you know."

"Oh, I know," Lux said. But she felt herself blushing.

"Of course you do," Emmett agreed, his dark eyes shining. And Lux realized she liked where she was for the first time in a long time. She didn't need her camera when she was with Emmett; she could look at him forever with both eyes wide open, instead of through a lens.

15

Back in her glass prison, also known as her father's apartment, Lux felt restless. Almost two weeks had passed since she'd left her mom's, and she and her father weren't speaking, which strangely made it easier for her to live with him. And so far, it seemed like Simone and her parents were all talk.

When she wasn't doing homework, Lux spent most of her time painting her nails, twisting her hair, or video-chatting with Emmett. She was still grounded, and the girls were still mad at her.

The one thing Lux looked forward to at the end of each day, oddly, was Penny.

"How was school?" Penny would ask when Lux pushed her way into the apartment each afternoon. Lux ignored her for days, until it became clear Penny wouldn't stop bugging her until she talked back.

"Fine," was all she said at first. But Penny kept asking Lux questions until she opened up.

Lux started helping Penny with Lillia, occasionally warming a bottle or grabbing the diaper cream, and though Lux still went quiet whenever her father was around, the afternoons before he got home from work—when it was just the three of them—became special.

"I found out three of my photos are going to run in the paper," Lux said one day, telling Penny something important for the first time without being asked first. Saying it out loud actually made her feel proud.

"Oh, that's wonderful, honey," Penny said back, and something in Lux's chest went warm when Penny called her honey. And the more Lux spoke to her, the more the glass prison started to feel like a home.

"There's a boy I think I like."

"Oh, really?" Genevieve asked. Lux had called her mom to tell her about Emmett because even though she and Penny were growing closer, she didn't feel comfortable telling her things like this. And she didn't have anyone else to talk to.

"I have some news for you, but tell me about him first," her mother said. So Lux did.

Her father and Penny walked into her room a few minutes into her gushing about Emmett. " . . . And he's an artist. He draws. And one of my photos that got picked for the paper was of him and his sketches."

When Lux saw her father standing in the doorway, she let her voice trail off, still fully committed to keeping the silent treatment going.

But he spoke first.

"I just got off the phone with Simone Harding's parents. They've decided not to move ahead with the assault charges because someone came forward and explained that Simone and her friends had been harassing you before and after the fight in the locker room."

"What?" Lux said, at the same time as Penny said, "I knew it."

"Wait, who came forward?" Lux said. She racked her brain, running through all the kids at her old school, and she couldn't imagine anyone being on her side, let alone caring enough to risk the wrath of Simone.

On the phone, her mother said, "I was going to tell you. It was a girl in your class. Daniella? Dayna?"

"Danika?" Lux asked.

"Yes. Her. She apparently told the school about how they'd been treating you and about things she'd seen online."

Her dad said, "The Hardings felt they had less of a case because of their daughter's actions and actually apologized for letting things go as far as they did."

Lux nodded slowly.

"This is good news, Luxana," her father said. "I'm still disappointed you lost control the way you did, and I don't ever want you to be involved with that kind of violence again. But I understand a little more now how and why things escalated. You're still grounded, but only until the end of the week."

Lux knew this was as close to an apology as she could expect from Luke. She smiled at him and nodded more, thinking about Danika's kindness. Lux hadn't spoken to her since she left her old school—she hadn't even replied to her messages—but Danika still had her back. Even after everything. She wrote Danika back then, thanking her for it all.

And that kind of loyalty gave Lux an idea.

—May 16—

I planned the whole prank myself.

I didn't know what Noelle, Tobyn, and Micah were planning to do for their junior-year prank because, of course, they hadn't told me after the truth came out. But I thought if I did something big, something to show I was sorry AND worthy of being a Flyy Girl, then maybe, just maybe, they'd forgive me for lying.

I was scared out of my mind that I'd get caught, but I thought that taking this risk could work in my favor, too. They'd see that I was willing to risk everything for their friendship . . . even going to military school.

I snuck into the school early in the morning and filled a bunch of plastic cups with water and carefully lined them up on the stairs that led to the Yard. All the cups were red except the ones I used to spell out I'M SORRY I LIED. The cups completely blocked the way, and no one could step down without knocking them over and spilling water everywhere, so when the students arrived, they lined up, took pictures, and laughed until the principal demanded that every student help pick up the cups until the stairs were clear.

So the girls would know that I did it, I also texted a selfie of me setting up the cups to all three of them with an apology:

Keep this to yourself, or turn me in. Just know I'm sorry and I'll never betray your trust again.

—A Wannabe Flyy Girl

Today, Noelle texted back.

Your secret's safe with us . . . so, wanna know what we're doing next?

Ashley Woodfolk has loved reading and writing for as long as she can remember. She graduated from Rutgers University with a Bachelor of Arts in English and worked in book publishing for ten years. She wrote her first novel, *The Beauty That Remains*, from a sunny Brooklyn apartment where she lives with her cute husband, her cuter dog, and the cutest baby in the world: her son Niko. *When You Were Everything* is her second novel, and Flyy Girls is her first fiction series.